To my dad, for all our countless hours of reading together;
and to my son Asa, ditto. — A. L. K.

For my beloved Nora. — C. V. A.

Text copyright © 2023 Aaron Lewis Krol
Illustrations copyright © 2023 Carlos Vélez Aguilera

First published in 2023 by Page Street Kids
an imprint of
Page Street Publishing Co.
27 Congress Street, Suite 1511
Salem, MA 01970
www.pagestreetpublishing.com

Distributed by Macmillan, sales in Canada by The Canadian Manda Group

23 24 25 26 27 CCO 5 4 3 2 1
ISBN-13: 978-1-64567-993-6
ISBN-10: 1-64567-993-4

CIP data for this book is available from the Library of Congress.

This book was typeset in PT Serif. The illustrations were done in mixed media.
Book design by Melia Parsloe for Page Street Kids
Cover design by Katie Beasley for Page Street Kids
Edited by Kayla Tostevin for Page Street Kids

Printed and bound in Shenzhen, Guangdong, China

Page Street Publishing uses only materials from suppliers who are committed to responsible
and sustainable forest management.

Page Street Publishing protects our planet by donating to nonprofits like The Trustees,
which focuses on local land conservation.

A Cloud in a Jar

written by Aaron Lewis Krol   illustrated by Carlos Vélez Aguilera

PAGE
STREET
KIDS

It was just after midnight on Walton Wharf West
When I heard someone rap on my window. "Psst! Hey!
I printed directions to Firelight Bay—
We're taking your rowboat, get dressed!"

And there was Lou Dozens, already halfway
Out the boathouse with oars and a vest.

On the Bay it was summer, twelve out of twelve months,
And children played tag down the world's longest slide
And had picnics on blankets a hundred yards wide
And all-year-round Easter egg hunts,

And at night watched the fireflies twinkle outside—
But they'd never seen rain, even once.

We were going to bring them a cloud in a jar,
So they could have showers, and rainbows, and stamp
Through puddles in big rubber boots, and get damp,
And run squealing from storms to the car.

The sea at our feet shone as bright as a lamp
And the Firelight Bay wasn't far.

But we'd hardly left shore when the wind at our tail
Started blowing so hard that our lunchboxes shook
And my scarf snapped about like a fish on a hook
As our boat stuttered into a gale!

I felt for Lou's hand, but she looked a keen look
And said, "*This* is a job—for a *SAIL*."

Then she leapt on the prow, where the wind whipped her hair
And she tossed me the cloud and reached into her sleeve,
Pulling dozens of handkerchiefs out in a weave
That she fanned out and knotted up square.

Her sheet caught the wind, and it started to heave,
And we sailed away, not knowing where.

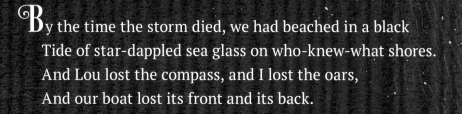

By the time the storm died, we had beached in a black
Tide of star-dappled sea glass on who-knew-what shores.
And Lou lost the compass, and I lost the oars,
And our boat lost its front and its back.

And beside us there, groaning like old wooden floors,
Was a *whale*, dragging sand in his track.

I looked up—and up—and I wiped off the wet
From my glasses to see the whale blow out a hot
Gust of seawater over the beach where he'd caught,
Every breath coming out in a jet.

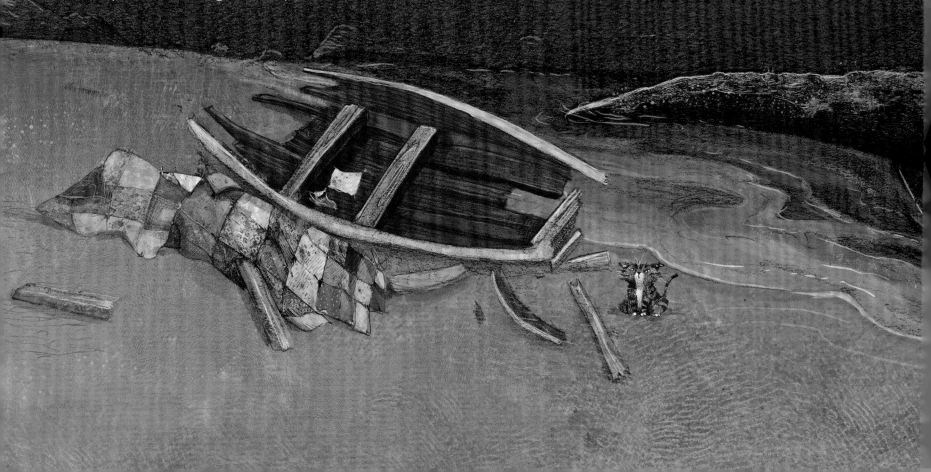

And Lou stroked her chin, and she thought a big thought,
And said, "*This* is a job—for a *NET*."

Then her fingers flicked through every inch of her coat,
Finding dozens of phone chargers balled up like twine
With prongs, tongs, and dongles in every design
Which she wove through the frame of our boat.

The whale wriggled in, and we hauled at the line,
And in no time we had him afloat!

Then—off! We were carried high over the spray,
So fast that the stars seemed to blur into snow.
And we watched our cloud rock in its jar, to and fro,
As we raced on to Firelight Bay.

But Lou put a hand to her ear, cautious, slow,
Like she'd heard someone call far away . . . .

A shadow swept over the stars like a shroud
And a black throng of razorbills blotted the sky!
And their skrackling, skreeling, cacophonous cry
Bore down on us, hungry and loud!

Lou reached for her sleeve, but I sighed a soft sigh
And said, "*This* is a job—for a *CLOUD*."

Then I held up the jar, and I gave it a twist,
And *POP!* went the lid as our cloud filled the night.
The razorbills shrieked, reeling back in midflight
In a whirlwind of moonlight and mist—

Through the clamor I heard Lou call out, "Hold on tight!"
And a hand grabbed ahold of my wrist . . . .

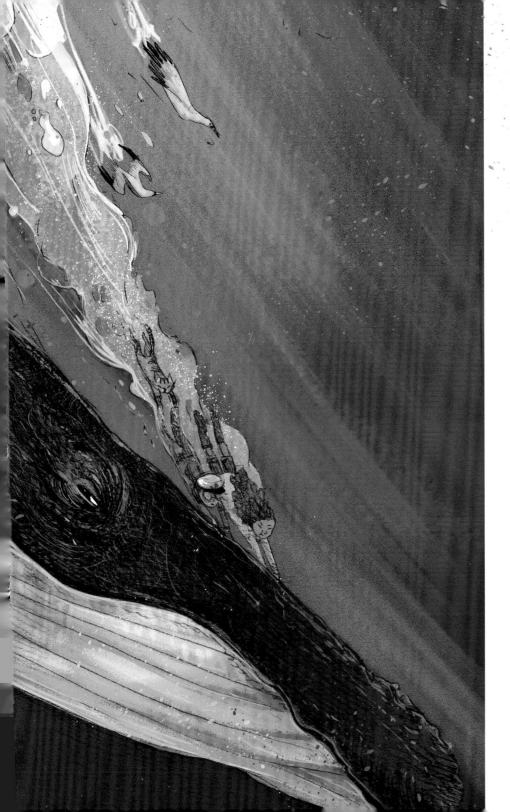

The sky seemed to *tilt*, and with one crashing roar
We dove through the onrushing tide and were gone!
I held a deep breath as the waves billowed on
Overhead for a mile or more.

And then—up we rose, in the first rays of dawn
Lighting down on a sea-speckled shore.

The whale thrummed with glee, catching sun on his tail,
  But I curled up and shivered, soaked through to my skin.
"It's the Bay!" shouted Lou as she scratched the whale's chin,
  But I sniffled and said, "But we failed."

And I pulled my vest tight as a breeze drifted in,
  Dragging wisps of our cloud in its trail.

But Lou wrung out her sleeves, and she grinned a sly grin,
And said, "*This* is a job—"

"For a *WHALE*."